FLAP YOUR WINGS AND TRY

BY CHARLOTTE POMERANTZ
ILLUSTRATED BY NANCY TAFURI

FLAP YOUR WINGS AND TRY

BY CHARLOTTE POMERANTZ
ILLUSTRATED BY NANCY TAFURI

GREENWILLOW BOOKS • NEW YORK

For Our Little Birds
Jessica · Caitlin · Lucas · Shani · Max
—C.P.
For All of Us Who Are Still Trying
—N.T.

Watercolor paints and a black pen were used for the
full-color art. The text type is ITC Bookman Light.

Text copyright © 1989 by Charlotte Pomerantz
Illustrations copyright © 1989 by Nancy Tafuri

Library of Congress Cataloging-in-Publication Data
Pomerantz, Charlotte.
Flap your wings and try / by Charlotte Pomerantz;
pictures by Nancy Tafuri.
p.   cm.
Summary: Following the advice of family members, a young bird
learns to fly and tells other birds that to fly, they need
only to flap their wings and try.
ISBN 0-688-08019-7.   ISBN 0-688-08020-0 (lib. bdg.)
[1. Birds—Fiction.   2. Flight—Fiction.   3. Growth—Fiction.
4. Stories in rhyme.]   I. Tafuri, Nancy, ill.   II. Title.
PZ8.3.P564F1 1989 [E]—dc 19 88-18766 CIP AC
Printed by SRA/McGraw-Hill.
Published by arrangement with HarperCollins Publisher's.

I'm a little baby bird
Wondering how to fly.
See my Grandma in the sky,
Why can't I, can't I.

See my Grandpa in the sky,
Why can't I, can't I.
Mommy whispers, Hushaby,
By and by you'll fly.

Daddy sings a lullaby,
By and by and by.

Sister says, Why don't you try,
Flap your wings and try.
So I flap my wings and try,

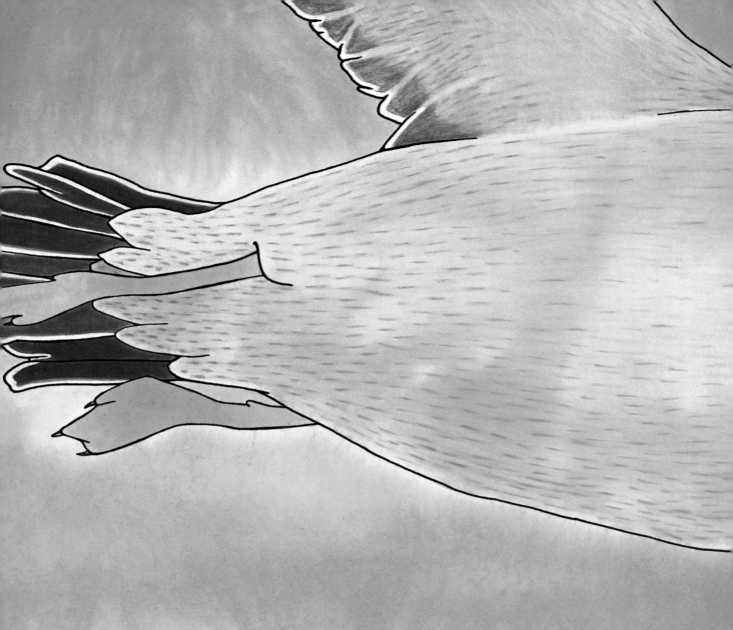

And soon I'm in the sky!
Look at me, way up high,
I can fly, can fly!

Below me is a baby bird.
She sees me in the sky.
I can almost hear her sigh,
Why can't I, can't I.

Down,
   down,
      down, way down I fly
And say, Why don't you try.

I watch her flap her wings
and try,

And soon she's in the sky!
Look at us, way up high,
We can fly, can fly!

Below us baby birds call, Why,
Why can't I, can't I.
Hush, we tell them, Hushaby,
You will fly, will fly.

You will fly,
by and by,
by and by and by.